Are you crazy about your pet?

Do you love cute and cuddly animals?

For budding doctors and nurses!

'I loved finding out how to help people.'
Beatrice, age 4

Perfect for fans of Holly Webb.

D0756076

C334230395

'Dr KittyCat is ready to rescue: Peanut the Mouse is exciting because you don't find out what's going to happen until the next chapter.'
Beatrice, age 4

'I enjoyed this book because I liked reading about Peanut being the patient for a change. That was funny and interesting and I read it from cover to cover!'
Persephone, age 7

A note from the author:

Jane says...

'When our guinea pig, Rosa, was recovering from an ear infection, she didn't want her usual favourite food (dandelion leaves). The only thing she wanted to eat was strawberry yogurt!'

Dr KittyCat really relies on her helpful assistant Peanut. In fact, she doesn't know what she'd do without him. So when Peanut is poorly, Dr KittyCat does all she can to make him feel better as quickly as possible!

For Dougal and Zebedee, my
first guinea pigs — J.C.

OXFORD
UNIVERSITY PRESS

Great Clarendon Street, Oxford OX2 6DP
Oxford University Press is a department of the University of Oxford.
It furthers the University's objective of excellence in research, scholarship,
and education by publishing worldwide

Oxford is a registered trade mark of Oxford University Press
in the UK and in certain other countries

Text © Jane Clarke and Oxford University Press 2018
Illustrations © Oxford University Press 2018

Cover artwork: Richard Byrne
Cover photograph: Rudmer Zwerver/Shutterstock.com
Inside artwork: Dynamo
All animal images from Shutterstock
With thanks to Christopher Tancock for advising on the first aid

The moral rights of the author/illustrator have been asserted

Database right Oxford University Press (maker)

First published in 2018

British Library Cataloguing in Publication Data

Data available

ISBN: 978-0-19-276599-4 (paperback)

2 4 6 8 10 9 7 5 3 1

Printed in China
Paper used in the production of this book is a natural,
recyclable product made from wood grown in sustainable forests.
The manufacturing process conforms to the environmental
regulations of the country of origin.

Dr KittyCat

is ready to rescue

Peanut the Mouse

Jane Clarke

OXFORD
UNIVERSITY PRESS

Chapter One

Peanut watched proudly as Dr KittyCat hung a framed certificate on the clinic wall. It said:

> This is to certify that
> Peanut the mouse has passed
> Advanced Furry First Aid
> and is now officially
> a Kind Carer.

Later, all the little animals were coming to a pizza and pyjama party to celebrate. They were going to make their own pizzas and have a sleepover in the vanbulance. Peanut couldn't wait!

But first, it was time for morning clinic. Peanut washed his paws and opened the door to the waiting room.

'Who's first in line to see Dr KittyCat today?' he squeaked.

A hamster wearing glasses and a bandana scampered in.

'Hello, Pumpkin,' said Peanut.

'Mm-mm!' Pumpkin mumbled. His face and neck looked very swollen.

Peanut glanced at him and then quickly leafed through the *Furry First-aid Book*.

'Dr KittyCat!' he squeaked. 'Swelling of the neck is a symptom of furry mumps. That's a very nasty infectious disease!'

'Don't panic, Peanut,' Dr KittyCat murmured. 'You'll scare our patient. Almost everyone is vaccinated against furry mumps when they're tiny, so it's rare for anyone to catch it. Pumpkin's eyes are nice and bright. He doesn't look very poorly to me.'

Pumpkin was trying to say something. 'Goo-ck!' he spluttered.

Peanut caught a glimpse of something orange behind the hamster's two front teeth.

Dr KittyCat soaped her paws and rinsed them carefully.

'You're safe in our paws,' she reassured Pumpkin. 'Let me take a look inside your mouth and find out what's going on.'

Pumpkin opened his mouth as wide as he possibly could.

'I can see straight away what the problem is,' Dr KittyCat purred. 'We'll have you feeling better in no time at all. Take a look, Peanut.'

Peanut peeped into Pumpkin's mouth.

'There's a piece of carrot wedged inside!' Peanut could see it pushing out Pumpkin's cheek pouches. 'That must be uncomfortable,' Peanut squeaked. 'We need to get it out!'

'Mwrrgh!' Pumpkin nodded his head in agreement.

Peanut went to the cupboard where the dental supplies were kept and took out a special sort of long, thin tweezers, called forceps. He handed the forceps to Dr KittyCat and watched as she gently extracted the piece of carrot. It took a bit of time to jiggle it out from behind Pumpkin's teeth.

'Thanks! That's much better.'
Pumpkin breathed a sigh of relief. 'I'll be more careful with the size of the food I stuff in my pouches from now on.' He rubbed his empty cheeks with his paws. 'May I have my piece of carrot back, please? I might want to nibble on it later.'

'Of course, but give your cheek pouches a rest and carry it home in your paw.' Dr KittyCat handed it to him. 'Well done, Pumpkin. You were very brave and kept still while I was removing it. You deserve a sticker.'

I was a purr-fect patient for Dr KittyCat!

Peanut handed him a sticker that said: 'I was a purr-fect patient for Dr KittyCat!' Pumpkin proudly stuck it on to his bandana.

'Thank goodness you don't have furry mumps. You would have had to miss my party!' Peanut told Pumpkin as he left. 'Don't forget your PJs!'

15

'I won't,' Pumpkin grinned. 'See you later.'

'Who's next?' Dr KittyCat asked as she and Peanut washed their paws ready for the next patient.

'Me!' Logan the puppy limped in. 'I have a sore toe,' he whimpered, holding out his poorly paw for Dr KittyCat to examine.

'Oh, poor Logan. It's hard to walk when you have a sore toe,' Dr KittyCat said sympathetically. 'But we can soon sort this out. A sharp piece of toenail is sticking into the toe next to it. You'll feel much better once your nails are clipped.'

She looked at Peanut and smiled. 'Peanut has his Kind Carer certificate now. He doesn't need to assist me this time. He can treat your paw all on his own.'

Peanut proudly fetched the big nail clippers. It felt good to be in charge of Logan's treatment. But the nail clippers were heavy for a little mouse.

He was tired by the time he had
finished clipping all sixteen of Logan's
toenails, and there were still several
patients to be seen . . .

At last, morning clinic was over. Peanut
wiped his forehead with his paw and sat
down to write up his notes.

'You worked very hard, and you were a great help this morning, Peanut,' Dr KittyCat said, taking out her knitting wool. She had some special sleepover pyjamas to knit. 'You are an excellent Kind Carer. I don't know what I'd do without you!'

Peanut gave a tired little smile. He opened the *Furry First-aid Book* and wrote down the name 'Pumpkin' and the date. Now, what had they treated Pumpkin for? It seemed such a long time ago. Peanut's head felt as if it was stuffed full of cotton wool. He stared at the paper. The words were swimming in front of his eyes. It was impossible to concentrate. All of a sudden, he felt drained of energy. The room and Dr KittyCat and her knitting seemed to be whirling around him. He stood up, but his legs were so wobbly they wouldn't take his weight. What was happening to him? Peanut gave a tiny squeak as the room went dark.

Chapter Two

Peanut opened his eyes. Dr KittyCat was kneeling next to him, holding his paw. Her flowery doctor's bag was beside her.

'Poor Peanut! You collapsed,' she murmured. 'Try not to worry. I'm right here. I saw you crumple to the ground. You didn't hit your head or anything.'

Dr KittyCat asked Peanut some simple questions to make sure he was not at all disorientated. He knew the answers to everything she asked him: the Queen's name, the date, the address of the clinic.

Peanut shivered. 'I'm so cold!' he cried.

Dr KittyCat put her cool paw on his forehead. 'You feel very warm,' she said. 'I think you might have a fever.'

She took the ear thermometer out of her bag and fitted it with a new hygiene cover. She gently inserted the thermometer in his ear and held it there until it went beep beep beep.

'Your temperature is higher than it should be . . .' Dr KittyCat murmured. 'Does anything hurt, Peanut?'

Peanut tried to sit up. He felt very dizzy, and he felt sore all over, from the whiskers on his nose to the tip of his tail.

'I ache!' he squeaked. 'And my throat hurts.'

'That's because your body is fighting some kind of infection,' Dr KittyCat told him.

'What kind of infection?' Peanut whimpered.

'I'm not sure yet. Infection is usually caused by bacteria or by a virus,' Dr KittyCat meowed. 'Or sometimes by fungi or parasites or mosquito bites . . .'

'Parasites?' Peanut shuddered.

He knew that parasites were things that lived inside you. Like worms.

'Sorry, Peanut, I was just thinking aloud.' Dr KittyCat frowned. 'You don't have any cuts, and you haven't been on holiday to any hot places. You always clean your paws before and after treating little animals . . .'

'What's wrong with me?' Peanut wailed.

'Don't panic, Peanut,' Dr KittyCat said gently. 'Even a little mouse who is always ready to rescue will need to be rescued himself sometimes. Now it's your turn to be the patient. I will work out what's wrong and help you get better, I promise. Let me examine you properly.'

She took Peanut by the paw and helped him up on the couch.

'Oww, my paws are sore,' Peanut groaned as he lay down.

'Are they?' Dr KittyCat picked up and examined each of his paws in turn.

'You have tiny spots on all your paws,' she told him. 'Let me check something . . .'

Dr KittyCat got up and came back with an empty glass. She pressed it down on the underside of one of Peanut's paw pads. 'The spots disappear when I apply pressure,' she murmured. 'That's good. It means they aren't caused by septicaemia—that's blood poisoning and it's very dangerous.'

'Daisy had spots on her paw when she had pawpox,' Peanut squeaked woozily.

'It's very unlikely to be pawpox,' Dr KittyCat told him. 'I remember you telling me that you had it when you were a little mouse. You don't get that twice. Now, let me check your chest and your ears, eyes, and throat.'

Dr KittyCat pressed her stethoscope to Peanut's furry chest and listened carefully.

'You have a good, strong heartbeat,' she commented. 'It's a little faster than usual, but that's to be expected . . .'

Dr KittyCat put a new cover on her otoscope and looked in Peanut's big, round ears. Her paws were very soft and gentle. *No wonder little animals feel safe when she comes to the rescue,* Peanut thought.

'Your ears are fine, Peanut,' Dr KittyCat said. 'There's no sign of infection in them. I'll take a good look at your eyes next.'

'I was having trouble reading before I collapsed,' Peanut groaned. Dr KittyCat carefully checked each of his eyes with her ophthalmoscope. She leaned in so close that Peanut could feel her whiskers brush his nose.

'Your eyes are a bit runny, but that's nothing to worry about,' she reassured him.

Peanut screwed up his eyes.

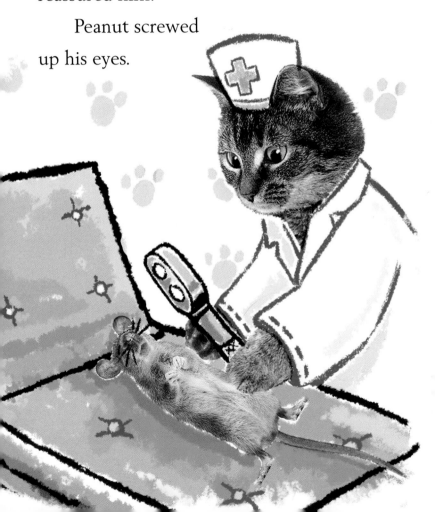

'Does this light hurt your eyes?' Dr KittyCat asked with concern. She shone the ophthalmoscope into his eyes again.

'No,' Peanut said. 'My eyes are just tired, that's all.'

'We're almost done,' said Dr KittyCat. 'Now, just follow the tip of my paw with your eyes but without moving your head.'

Peanut watched the furry paw move slowly in all directions and managed to keep absolutely still.

'Is your neck stiff? Try bending it.' She gently helped Peanut to sit up.

'My neck is OK,' Peanut said. He vaguely remembered from his

furry first-aid exam that Dr KittyCat
was making sure he didn't have a
dangerous disease called men . . . men
. . . meningitis. His brain was working
slower than usual. 'I feel dizzy,' he
groaned as he lay back down.

'You're doing very well,
Peanut,' Dr KittyCat
purred. 'I think I know
what is wrong with
you now.

I just need you to be brave a tiny bit longer while I check inside your mouth. I'll need a good light for that.'

Dr KittyCat reached into her bag and put on her surgical headlamp. She clicked it on and took a disposable wooden tongue depressor out of a packet. It looked like a big flat ice-lolly stick.

'Urk!' Peanut gagged as she gently held down his tongue.

'Try to relax and breathe deeply, Peanut,' Dr KittyCat advised.

Peanut breathed slowly in and out.

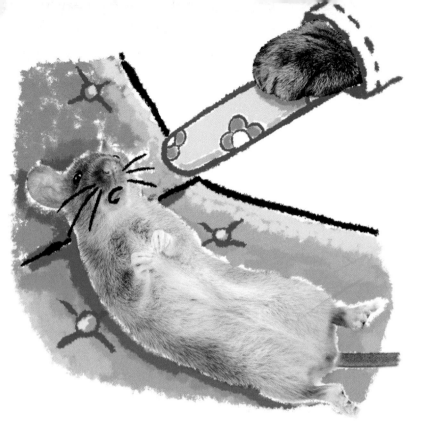

He tried to relax and think of cheese,
but he didn't feel hungry at all.

'All finished, Peanut!' Dr KittyCat
told him. 'I can see your throat is sore,
but the airway is clear. You have tiny
spots around the edges of your tongue

and on the inside of your mouth, and
that makes me sure of my diagnosis. I'm
happy to say you're not seriously ill. But
you do have a nasty case of paw and
jaw disease.'

'Paw and jaw disease?' Peanut
mumbled. He couldn't remember
learning about that.

'I'm afraid so,' Dr KittyCat was
saying. 'It is infectious, so we will have
to postpone your pizza and pyjama
party.'

Peanut felt too poorly to be upset.

'I'll get you settled in your bed in
the vanbulance and give you something
to help with the aches and pains and

fever.' Dr KittyCat scooped up her little mouse assistant in her arms. 'You'll need me to look after you for a few days until you feel better.'

Peanut closed his eyes. 'I feel safe in your paws,' he squeaked.

Chapter Three

The vanbulance rumbled with the gentle sound of mouse snores. Peanut was sleeping peacefully, thanks to the special medicine Dr KittyCat had given him. Dr KittyCat put a jug of water and a glass beside his bed and hurried back to the clinic. There was an awful lot to do. First, she rushed around, packing

things away and
wiping down the
surfaces to get
rid of any germs.
Then, she washed
her paws and picked up
the old-fashioned telephone.

She called Mrs Hazelnut, who
was looking after the little animals at
lunch club. 'Peanut is poorly,' she said.
'We'll have to put off tonight's pizza
and pyjama party until he's better.
Please tell everyone there's been a
change of plan. I'll be holding a special
"crafternoon" at the clinic from 3.30 to
5p.m. instead.'

Dr KittyCat put down the phone and pulled out a box full of craft supplies. It wasn't long before the little animals began to arrive.

'Can we go and visit Peanut in the vanbulance?' Nutmeg the guinea pig asked.

'Peanut can't have any visitors yet,' Dr KittyCat told them all. 'He needs peace and quiet and a good rest, and we don't want him to infect anyone else with paw and jaw disease.'

'Logan and I saw him at the clinic this morning,' said Pumpkin, sounding worried. 'Does that mean we'll get paw and jaw too?'

'I hope not,' Dr KittyCat replied, smiling. 'Fortunately, paw and jaw isn't as infectious as pawpox, and Peanut is always very careful to clean his paws

between patients. We will find out
between three and six days from now
if anyone is going to catch paw and jaw
from him.'

The little animals looked at one
another a bit uncertainly.

'If you meet someone with paw
and jaw, you could get the disease

yourself any time between three and six days afterwards. It's called the incubation period,' Dr KittyCat explained. 'It's different for different diseases. If six days pass and no one else in Thistletown catches paw and jaw, then we don't need to worry about it any longer.'

'Whoo-oo did Peanut catch it from?' hooted Sage the owlet.

'No one else in Thistletown has it,' Dr KittyCat meowed thoughtfully. 'The only time Peanut's been out of Thistletown was when he did the Kind Carer exam in Pondlake City. Furry first-aiders from around the country were there. And that was on Monday. Four days ago! So perhaps I'll phone the organizers to let them know about Peanut and check whether anyone else is ill.'

'I don't want to catch paw and jaw,' Daisy shuddered. 'I remember how horrid it was to have pawpox. That was enough for me.'

'Peanut will be better in a few days, but, right now, he is feeling very poorly and sorry for himself,' Dr KittyCat said, 'which is why I thought we could make him a great big get-well-soon card to cheer him up.' She pulled out an enormous sheet of card and folded it in half. 'Now, what shall we draw on the card?' she wondered aloud.

'Peanut likes lots of different types of cheese,' Sage suggested.

'I'll cut out a triangle and colour it like a wedge of cheese and stick it on the card!' squeaked Nutmeg.

'So will I! And me! And me!' clamoured the little animals.

'You can all do one,' Dr KittyCat told them, smiling.

'I'll cover mine in paw prints,' yapped Logan.

'I'll stick on cut-out flowers, like the ones on my necklace,' said Daisy.

'I'll use sequins!' woofed Posy.

'I'll draw carrots!' squealed Pumpkin.

'And I'll stick on feathers!' quacked Willow.

There was a kerfuffle as the little animals dived into the craft box for supplies.

'Owww!' howled Ginger the kitten and Fennel the fox cub as they bumped heads.

'Please be careful,' Dr KittyCat warned them, but in no time at all there was a loud meow! Dr KittyCat hurried over to Daisy.

A tiny drop of blood dripped from the kitten's paw and plopped on to one of her cut-out paper flowers. Dr KittyCat looked at the plastic scissors Daisy was using. 'How did you cut yourself with those?' she asked, puzzled.

'The paper cut me, not the scissors,' Daisy meowed.

Dr KittyCat led her to the sink to wash her paw.

'Paper cuts are horrid,' she said sympathetically. She carefully patted Daisy's paw dry with a piece of clean gauze. 'Which sticking plaster would you like?' she asked.

'That one.'
Daisy pointed to a
sticking plaster with
flowers on it.

Just as Dr KittyCat was carefully
cleaning up the drip of Daisy's blood,
there was a sudden atchooo-ouch! Posy
was shaking her head from side to side.

Choo, too, choo! she sneezed.

'Are you allergic to something,
Posy?' Dr KittyCat asked the little
puppy.

'Sequins!' sneezed Posy. 'One got
stuck up my nose.'

Dr KittyCat cleaned her paws and
took a look.

'I can see it!' She took out her sterile tweezers. The little animals stopped what they were doing to watch.

'Never try to do this yourself,' Dr KittyCat warned. 'If you get anything stuck in a nose or an ear you must see a doctor or first-aider.'

I was a purr-fect patient for Dr KittyCat!

Posy stood very still as Dr KittyCat carefully extracted the sequin.

'Be very careful not to snuffle up any more sequins,' she told Posy.

'I will be!' woofed Posy. 'Please may I have a sticker?'

'Of course.' Dr KittyCat found Posy a sticker. There was a tap on her shoulder.

'You forgot to give me mine,' meowed Daisy.

From the corner of the room came a loud qua-a-ack! Willow had poured a jar of glue all over herself, and her feathers were all stuck together.

'Keep calm,' Dr KittyCat meowed.
'I'll be there in a whisker . . .'

'Well done, everyone,' Dr KittyCat said
as she waved them goodbye. 'You made
a wonderful get-well card for Peanut.
I'm sure it will cheer him up when he
sees it. Have a good weekend!'

Dr KittyCat looked at the mess and
sighed. Then she rolled up the sleeves
of her doctor's coat and cleaned up the
sticky mess and paw prints. She really
missed the help of her kind and caring
first-aid assistant. She just had time to
make the precautionary call to Pondlake

City before picking up the *Furry First-aid Book* and making her way back to the vanbulance.

Peanut was still fast asleep in his little cabin. 'Get well soon, Peanut,' Dr KittyCat whispered, closing his curtains. She sat down on her paw-print bedspread and began to write up the furry first-aid notes of the day. There were so many that she dozed off before she could finish them.

Chapter Four

Dr KittyCat sat bolt upright in her bed. What had woken her at three o'clock in the morning? Why was she still wearing her doctor's coat? And why were there sequins stuck to her stripy tail?

'Dr KittyCat!' Peanut croaked. 'I need a drink of water and some more medicine!'

'Peanut!' Dr KittyCat leaped out of bed and checked Peanut's temperature. 'It's going down,' she purred. She poured a mouse-sized teaspoon of medicine. Peanut opened his mouth a little way then shut it so suddenly that the sticky medicine spilled all over Dr KittyCat's silvery fur.

'My mouth's really sore,' he wailed.

'Poor Peanut,' Dr KittyCat comforted him. 'It will get better in a day or two. Try some soothing mouth gel for that.' She squeezed a little on to Peanut's paw. 'Massage it on the sore spots,' she told him. 'That's right.'

She filled a glass with water and helped him take a sip.

'Now, let's try that spoonful of medicine again,' she said, pouring another spoonful. This time, Peanut was able to swallow it.

'That's a good little mouse,' Dr KittyCat murmured as they both fell back to sleep.

In the morning, Dr KittyCat managed to wash herself before Peanut woke up. Once he was awake, she showed him the huge card the little animals had made.

Inside it said:

Get well, Peanut! We miss our kind carer.

'Everyone decorated triangles like pieces of cheese for the front and put their mark on the inside,' Dr KittyCat told him.

Peanut couldn't help smiling at the card, even though it made his mouth hurt.

Dr KittyCat fetched her flowery doctor's bag.

'Are you feeling a bit better today?' Dr KittyCat asked Peanut as she put the thermometer back in her bag. 'Your temperature is almost back to normal.'

'I'm not shivery any more,' Peanut squeaked, 'and my head feels a lot less woozy.' He swung his feet out of bed.

'My legs are still wobbly,' he groaned. He stared at the marks on his paws. 'Oh no! The spots are getting worse!' he squeaked.

'It's normal for spots to get brighter before they fade,' Dr KittyCat reassured him. 'Stay in bed today. We need to keep you warm and quiet and make sure you drink plenty of liquids.'

She looked inside Peanut's mouth.

'Those spots do look sore,' she said sympathetically. She handed him the soothing gel.

'You can use this whenever you need to.'

Peanut rubbed the gel on to the sore spots in his mouth. It tasted minty and fresh.

'I found a straw while you were asleep,' Dr KittyCat went on. 'This should make it a bit easier to drink.'

Peanut sucked up a big refreshing mouthful of water.

'You should try to eat something today too,' Dr KittyCat advised. 'It will help you get your strength back. Is there anything you'd like to eat? How about some of your favourite cheese?'

'I don't feel hungry at all,' Peanut moaned. 'I just want to feel better straight away.'

'I'll get my knitting and sit beside you.' Dr KittyCat took out her wool and her knitting needles. She was using two colours and knitting something stripy. Peanut wondered if it might be something for him. He wasn't always a big fan of Dr KittyCat's creations. He closed his eyes. He felt too weak to even groan.

At lunchtime, Dr KittyCat made cheese and broccoli soup. She held a spoonful up to Peanut's mouth.

Peanut stared at it in disgust. 'Yuck! There are green bits in it.'

'Try a little bit,' Dr KittyCat coaxed, but Peanut turned his head away.

At teatime, Dr KittyCat made cheese and onion soup.

Peanut tightened his lips. There were brown bits floating on the top of the soup. He didn't want to taste that either. 'No, thanks,' he said.

At dinner time, Dr KittyCat made cheese soup.

'It's only got cheese and milk in it!' she told him. Peanut managed a tiny bit.

'Well done, Peanut!' Dr KittyCat said, smiling. 'Now, how about some fruit?' She cut an apple into tiny pieces.

'It's too crunchy,' Peanut mumbled. 'It will hurt my mouth.'

'I'll cook it into apple sauce. I'll be back in a whisker!'

Dr KittyCat returned with some warm apple sauce.

'It's too mushy,' Peanut moaned,

but he did manage to eat a couple of mouse-sized spoonfuls.

Dr KittyCat checked Peanut's temperature again and smiled. 'You're on the road to recovery,' she told him. Then they both settled down for a sleep.

Chapter
Five

It was a whole week later, and Peanut was feeling much better.

'No one else has caught paw and jaw,' Dr KittyCat meowed when she popped in to the vanbulance to see Peanut during her morning break. 'Your spots have faded and you're not infectious any more, so you can come back to the clinic this afternoon!'

'Yay!' Peanut squeaked.

Dr KittyCat's looking tired, Peanut thought. *I hope that's not because of me.* He'd been wandering around the vanbulance at all hours of the day and night, helping himself to cheese and crackers and fizzy drinks, but he didn't think she'd noticed.

That afternoon he made his way over to the clinic. It was good to be back. 'I'll check the contents of your bag to make sure we are ready to rescue!' he told Dr KittyCat. 'Paw-cleansing gel, wipes, thermometer, stethoscope, surgical headlamp,'

he murmured, 'ophthalmoscope,
otoscope, tongue depressors, tweezers,
scissors, syringe, magnifying glass,
bandages, sticking plasters, tape, gauze,
instant cool packs, peppermint lozenges,
medicines, dental mirror, ointments,
clinical waste bag, reward stickers . . .'

Peanut frowned. 'Something's missing,' he squeaked.

'Mouth gel,' Dr KittyCat said, smiling. 'We used that all up on you.' She reached into the supplies cupboard and handed Peanut a new tube.

'Now we're ready to rescue again!' she meowed.

Peanut sat down at his desk. He opened the *Furry First-aid Book* to the page about paw and jaw disease. *Occasionally causes fingernails and toenails to drop off, but they grow back,* he read. *Very rarely, serious complications occur.*

Eek, Peanut thought. *What if I get serious complications?*

Dr KittyCat noticed what he was reading. 'It's not a good idea to read everything about a disease you have,' she told him. 'It causes a lot of unnecessary worry. Let your doctor look out for you.'

'I'm glad you're my doctor!' Peanut sighed with relief. He found his pencil and began to sort through the patient notes that Dr KittyCat had scribbled on loose pieces of paper. Dr KittyCat's handwriting was quite hard to read, and they all needed entering in the book.

Dr KittyCat sat down and reached

for her knitting.

'I didn't realize how much you helped around here until you were ill,' she purred. 'I'm so glad you are back!'

'Before I got ill, I didn't realize what it's like to be a patient,' Peanut squeaked. 'Our purr-fect patients really deserve their stickers!'

'That reminds me!' Dr KittyCat got up and fetched the sticker box. She took one out, crossed out 'purr-fect', and put a smiley face on it.

'You're a much better Kind Carer than you are a patient,' she said,

I was a ~~purr-fect~~ :) patient for Dr KittyCat!

laughing as she gave it to Peanut.

'It's hard to be a patient patient,' Peanut replied, giggling.

Hee hee heii-hic!

His giggle turned into hiccups.

Ee-hic-eek! he squeaked. 'I've got serious complic-*hic*-ations!'

He looked at Dr KittyCat. She was trying not to smile.

Ee-hic-eek!

'Serious complications for paw and jaw disease are worsening fever, a stiff neck, and back pain, *not* hiccups!' she told him. 'Don't panic, Peanut. Everyone gets hiccups from time to time. It's nothing to be worried about. You'll be fine!'

Peanut hiccuped gently to himself as he wrote up the notes. It took him quite a while.

'Shouldn't the hiccups have—*hic*—stopped by now—*hic*?' he asked.

'Hiccups almost always stop on their own,' Dr KittyCat reassured him. 'They aren't a problem as long as they don't go on longer than forty-eight hours.'

'Forty-eight—*hic*—hours? That's—*hic*—two days!' Peanut squeaked.

'There are a few things you can try,' Dr KittyCat said, 'like taking little sips of cold water.'

Peanut fetched himself a glass of water and took tiny sips until it was empty, but he still had the hiccups.

'Try holding your breath and counting,' Dr KittyCat suggested.

Peanut sucked in some air and counted the seconds in his head.

. . . *Thirty-one, thirty-two, thirty—hic! Hi-hic!*

'Hiccups come from contractions of your diaphragm,' Dr KittyCat explained. 'That's the big muscle at the bottom of your chest that helps you breathe. Try compressing it by pulling your knees up to your chest.'

Peanut did as Dr KittyCat instructed. 'That's not—*hic*—working either,' Peanut grumbled.

'Never mind, Peanut,' Dr Kitty said. 'You need something to take your mind off it. Let's decorate the

vanbulance. Your pizza and pyjama
party can go ahead this evening.
I've called everyone to let them know.
And, look, I've knitted you a new pair
of PJs!'

Dr KittyCat held up a pair of
knitted candy-striped pyjamas.

'For me?' Peanut gave a great
gasp. 'Oh! I've stopped hiccuping!' he
exclaimed.

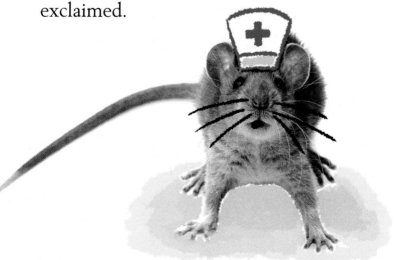

'That's good.' Dr KittyCat looked
a bit puzzled. 'They say a scare can stop
hiccups, but you're not scared of a pair
of knitted pyjamas, are you?'

'I'm a bit scared to wear them,' Peanut admitted. 'I . . . er . . . might get them covered in tomato sauce when we make pizza.'

'Don't panic, Peanut,' purred Dr KittyCat. 'They'll wash!'

Chapter Six

A group of little animals wearing pyjamas crowded round the fold-out table in the vanbulance. They were putting toppings on their pizzas.

'This is fun!' Peanut exclaimed as he covered his pizza base in cherry tomatoes.

'Your pizza looks as if it's covered in spots, like you were,' Daisy meowed.

'My spots were flat, not bumpy,' Peanut told her.

'Well, my pawpox spots were bumpy,' Daisy replied, sprinkling slices of olives on her pizza.

'I hate olives!' Ginger wrinkled her nose. 'But I like peppers. Especially hot ones.' She put a big chilli pepper in the middle of her pizza.

Posy pointed to Logan, Sage, and Fennel's pizzas. 'Copycats!' she woofed. Like her, they'd covered their pizzas in slices of ham.

Pumpkin wiped a splat of tomato paste off his glasses. 'I think seeds are the best topping for pizza,' he said.

'I agree!' wheeped Nutmeg.

'Does anyone want cheese on top?' Dr KittyCat asked.

'Yes, please!' they all shouted.

Dr KittyCat carefully placed
the pizzas in the oven, and soon the
vanbulance was filled with a wonderful
aroma.

'Yum!' the little animals squeaked as Dr KittyCat took the pizzas out of the oven.

'Don't eat too fast. You'll get hiccups!' Peanut advised them as they waited for the pizzas to cool.

'Willow and I won't,' Sage hooted smugly. 'Birds don't get hiccups.'

'Don't they?' Peanut wondered, looking at Dr KittyCat.

'They don't!' confirmed Dr KittyCat.

The little animals tucked in. Soon, Pumpkin's pouches were bulging.

'It's OK,' he mumbled. 'Nothing's stuck in them. I'm just saving some pizza for later.'

Dr KittyCat clapped her paws.
Everyone fell silent. Posy gave a big
hiccup, but only one.

'This party is for my brilliant
assistant, Peanut,' Dr KittyCat said.
'I'm so happy that he's well again. As
you know, he is now officially a Kind
Carer. Congratulations, Peanut. We
are all very proud of you!' She handed

him a mouse-sized copy of the framed
certificate that hung on the clinic wall.

Everyone gave him a big round of
applause.

Peanut's ears went bright pink.
'Thank you, everyone,' he squeaked.
'And thank you, Dr KittyCat, for
looking after me when I was ill—and
for knitting my special party pyjamas!'

'I knew you'd
love them!'
Dr KittyCat
said.

Then she gave an enormous yawn
that showed her gleaming white teeth.
'No one ever gets much sleep at a
sleepover,' she purred. 'I'm off
to curl up on a nice quiet
couch in the clinic. Have
fun!'

'We will!' Peanut
assured her.

'Call me if you need me,'
Dr KittyCat told him. 'I'm always
ready to rescue!'

The end

Dr KittyCat's top ten tips for helping someone get over an infection:

1. Make sure the poorly person has plenty of extra rest.

2. Make sure they are always comfortable.

3. Drinking plenty of fluids is important, and warm drinks can be soothing.

4. If any medicines have been prescribed by a doctor, make sure the patient takes them as instructed.

5. Don't let the patient get too hot or too cold.

6. A supply of books, quiet music, or a favourite film to watch can help.

7. The patient may not have much of an appetite, but do encourage them to eat nutritious foods to help them fight the infection.

8. Comfort and company can go a long way to make a poorly person feel better!

9. Make sure the patient has a good supply of disposable tissues for blowing their nose or covering coughs and sneezes.

10. If you're the one looking after a poorly person, make sure you get enough rest too!

If you loved Peanut the Mouse, here's an extract from another Dr KittyCat adventure:

Dr KittyCat is ready to rescue: Logan the Puppy

This time Dr KittyCat is helping a puppy called Logan who has grazed himself on the way to the swimming pool . . .

Peanut took an instant cool pack out of Dr KittyCat's bag. He twisted the bag until he felt the inner bag burst. Then he shook it up and down and side to side until he felt the contents go ice-cold. He handed it to Dr KittyCat.

Dr KittyCat gently pressed the icy pack against the bruised area on Logan's tail. 'Is that a bit better?' she asked Logan.

'A tiny bit.' Logan's shoulders shuddered.

'Where did the blood come from if it didn't come from Logan's tail?' asked Peanut, frowning. Then he turned to the little animals. 'Are you all OK?' he asked. Everyone nodded their heads.

Here are some other stories that we think you'll love!